To Auntie Pat, a real tough Cookie

Tough Cookie

DAVID WISNIEWSKI

LOTHROP, LEE & SHEPARD BOOKS

NEW YORK

JTA WELCOME

The Jar Transit Authority welcomes you to the Jar and hopes that the following information makes your stay safer and more enjoyable.

Please remember to carry your ID card and sell-by date with you at all times. Freshness determines your level within the Jar. It's the law!

When your sell-by date expires, please report to the nearest processing center for clearance to the next level down.

Those assigned to the Bottom of the Jar no longer need report to a processing center.

Crumbs will not be issued ID cards and must remain at the Bottom of the Jar.

WANTED
BY THE JAR POLICE DEPT.

FOR ASSAULT AND BATTERY
FINGERS
CONSIDERED ARMED AND DANGEROUS

TO THE JAR!

THE LID
As there may be sudden movement at any time, please avoid this area after your initial entry.

SKYNET AND PROCESSING CENTER
After a cushioned fall, new arrivals are assigned living space based on freshness and quality.

UPJAR
This exclusive neighborhood is home to just-baked and best-quality store-bought citizens.

CROCKER OBSERVATORY
This state-of-the-art facility monitors Lid movement.

MIDJAR
This level is the site of major business, cultural, and government centers.

THE ELS
These elevators connect Midjar to Upjar.

DOWNJAR
Most shops, services, schools, and apartment buildings are located here.

PILLSBURY EXPRESSWAY
This excellent highway system also features convenient bus service.

THE BOTTOM OF THE JAR
Visitors to this area should travel in groups.

They call me a tough cookie. I guess I am.
  Came from a regular batch. Lots of dough. Lived the high
life. Top of the Jar. Then I hit bottom and stayed here. It was
rough. Still is. But you get used to it.
  Life's still sweet. Just a little stale.

The bottom's loaded with nice folks. Some call them crumbs. I call them friends. I like helping them out. Anybody makes trouble, I step in.

That's my job. I'm a tough cookie.

I'm knocking back a cup of java when this classy blond rolls
up. Store-bought. Easy on the eyes. "Pecan Sandy," I say.
"Long time."
"Better that way," she says.
We used to be an item. Didn't work. Still hurts.
"So what's up?" I mutter.

She chokes back a sob. "Your partner. . ."
My raisins turn to ice. "Chips?"
She's crying now. "Fingers got him."
I grab her arm. "Where?"
"Crossjar," she says, getting a grip. This cookie don't crumble. "Cab's outside."

Chips and I go way back. Entered the Jar the same time. Joined the force together. Became partners. We were good. Busted the Ginger Snaps. Broke up the Macaroons. But then...

They're loading him when we get there. He's chewed up pretty bad. I take his hand. "Chips," I say.

He opens his eyes. Gasps. "Fingers...looking for you."

Shock jolts my gut, but I don't let it show. "Fingers don't come this far down."

"Did this time," groans Chips.

I squeeze his hand. "You're a tough cookie. You'll make it."

He closes his eyes. "Yeah," he mumbles. "I'll make it."

They take him away.

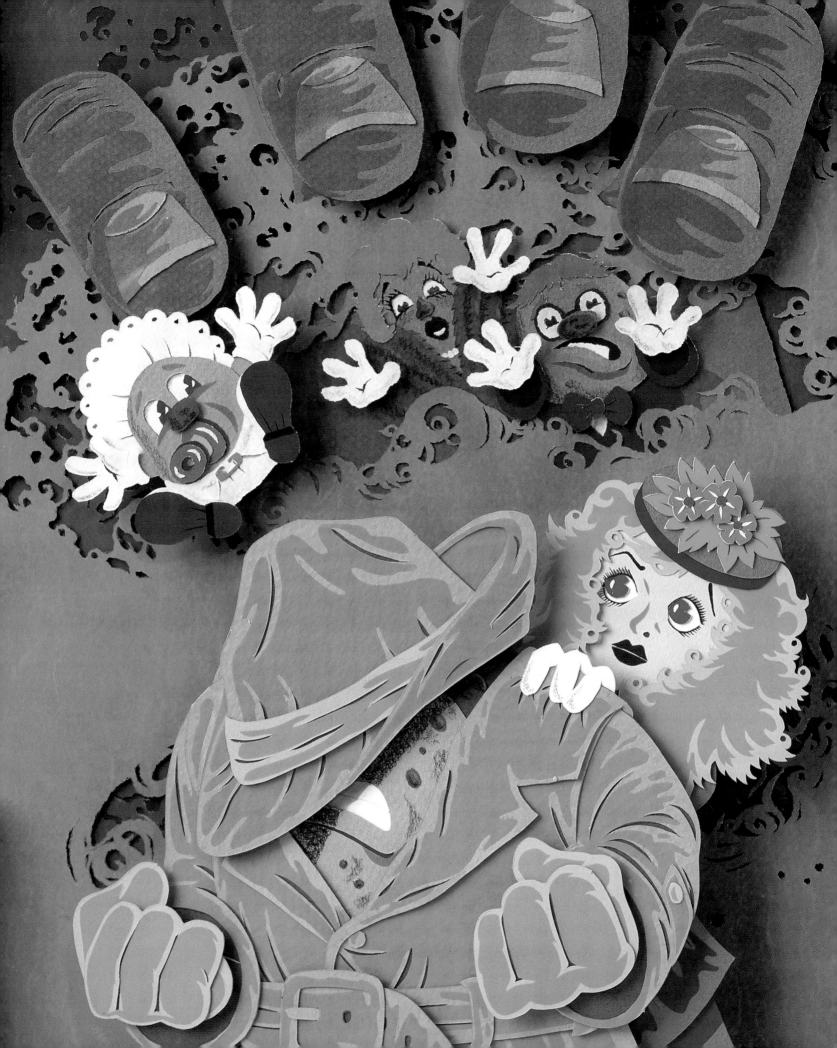

Standing in the cold night, a hot flood of memory hijacks my brain. Mom. Dad. The Top of the Jar. The knock at the door. Fingers. . .

And later. Me and Chips. The Pfeffernuesse case. Tried to save them. Couldn't.

Fingers. . .FINGERS!

A slap stings my cheek like a velvet bee. "Snap out of it!" pipes Pecan Sandy. "You can't run anymore. You're such a tough cookie? Prove it!"

"You're right," I say. "Time to put Fingers away. For keeps."

At the police station, the chief offers nothing but lousy coffee and bad advice. "Forget about it, son," he says. "You can't stop Fingers."

Other cops gather around. They look big. They talk tough. But inside, they're marshmallows. "That's right," they mumble. "Nobody stops Fingers."

"We'll see about that," I say.

Crumbs are waiting outside. Word travels fast.
"We owe you big-time," says one. "Let us help."
The others nod.
Their faces blur. It gets hard to talk. I look away. "Thanks,"
I say, "but no thanks. This is between Fingers and me."

It's a long ride to the Top of the Jar. I begin to think maybe I'm a nutbar to do this. Then I think of Chips. . .

The doors open. Everything's fresh and warm. I grab the first guy I see. "Hey, Gumdrop," I say. "Where's Fingers?"

The guy can't take the pressure. Starts to snap. "I don't know!" he squeals.

That's when the trouble starts. The Jar shakes. The sky opens.

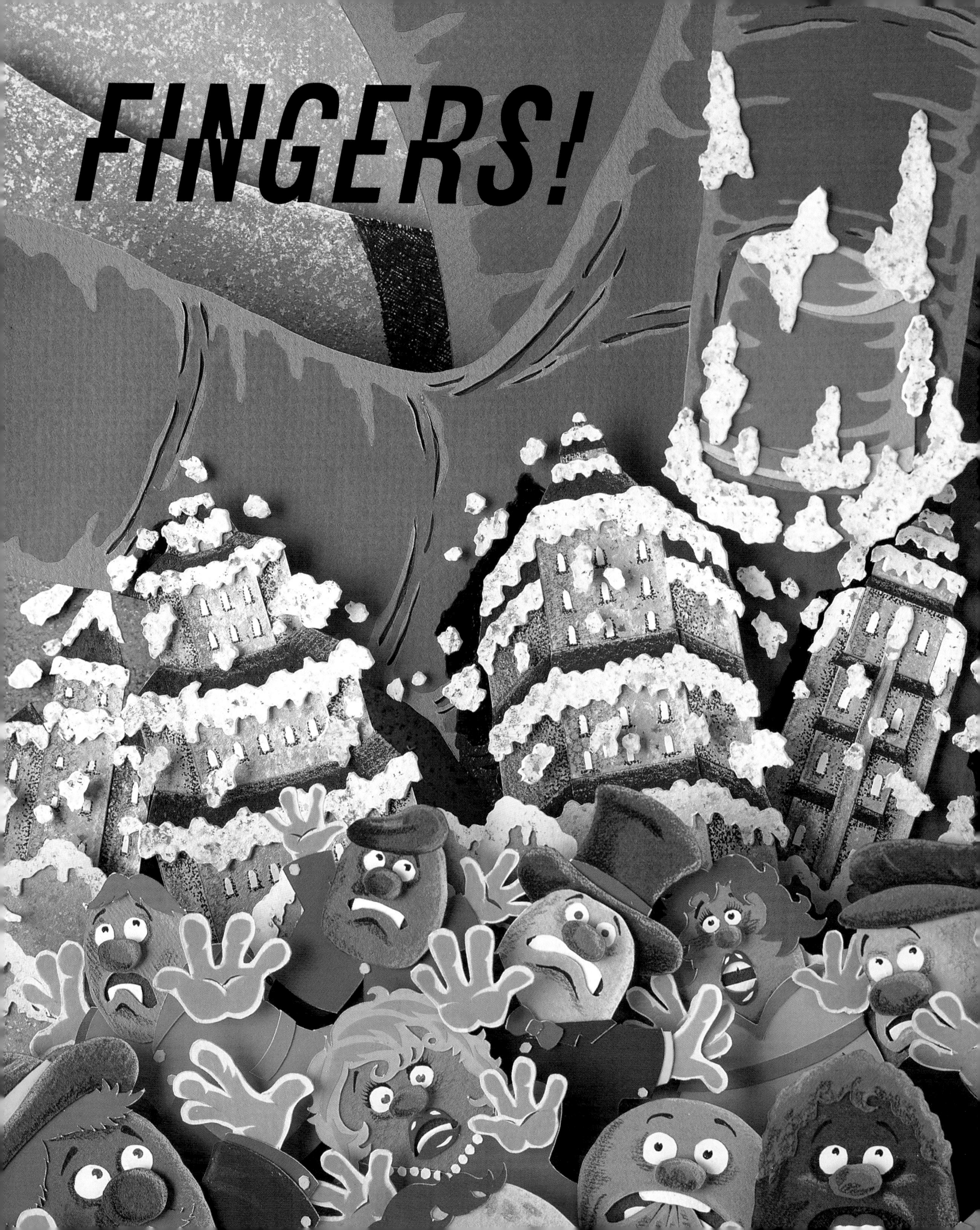
FINGERS!

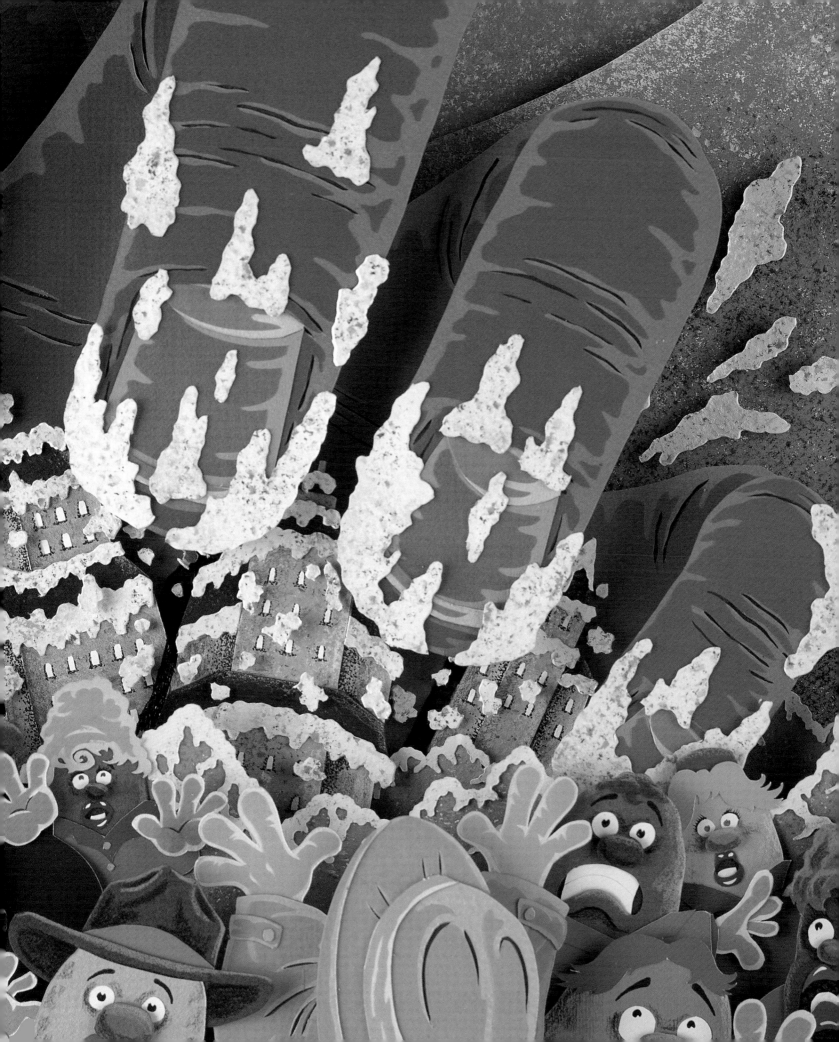

Gumdrop's the first to go. A couple of shortbreads get it next.
Then Fingers heads toward yours truly. Darkness covers me like
a damp sponge. Can't move. Can't breathe. It's the end. . .

Then the doors open. Pecan Sandy strides in, followed by every crumb in the Jar. They lay on Fingers by the hundreds, the thousands!

Fingers gives them the brush-off and makes another grab, but more crumbs join the fracas. Again and again, Fingers gets nothing but crumbs.

Finally, it's over.

Pecan Sandy sidles over and helps me up. "I figured Fingers was only after cookies," she says. "All he got was crumbs."

I kiss her. "You're a smart cookie," I say. "Maybe being a tough cookie isn't enough."

She kisses me. "You don't learn quick," she says, "but you learn."

THE END

Color-Aid and Strathmore watercolor papers were used for the full-color illustrations. Photography of cut-paper illustrations by Studio One. The text type is 16-point Gill Sans Bold. Copyright © 1999 by David Wisniewski. All rights reserved. No part of this book may be reproduced or utilized in any form or by any means, electronic or mechanical, including photocopying, recording, or by any information storage and retrieval system, without permission in writing from the Publisher. Published by Lothrop, Lee & Shepard Books, a division of William Morrow and Company, Inc. 1350 Avenue of the Americas, New York, NY 10019. www.williammorrow.com

Printed in Singapore at Tien Wah Press. 10 9 8 7 6 5 4 3 2 1

Library of Congress Cataloging-in-Publication Data
Wisniewski, David. Tough cookie/David Wisniewski.
p. cm. Summary: When his friend Chips is snatched and chewed, Tough Cookie sets out to stop Fingers.
ISBN 0-688-15337-2 (trade)—ISBN 0-688-15338-0 (library) [1. Cookies—Fiction. 2. Humorous stories.] I. Title. PZ7.W78036To 1999 [E]—dc21 98-45188 CIP AC